Bible Verses for Military Life

God's Word for
Protection, Power, and Perseverance

Nancy DeJesus

Author and Photographer

D1608191

The use of images depicting United States armed forces does not imply or constitute Department of Defense endorsement.

Cover illustration by Nancy DeJesus.

All scripture quotations are taken from the following public domain Holy Bible translations: World English Bible (WEB), World Messianic Bible (WMB), Open English Bible (OEB), Bible in Basic English (BBE).

ISBN: 9798560113933

CONTENTS

Introduction

Don't be afraid, and don't be dismayed because of this great multitude; for the battle is not yours, but God's.
2 Chronicles 20:15

He gives power to the weak. He increases the strength of him who has no might. Even the youths faint and get weary, and the young men utterly fall; but those who wait for the Lord will renew their strength. They will mount up with wings like eagles. They will run, and not be weary. They will walk, and not faint.
Isaiah 40:29-31

I wrote this book for all members of the military: active, reserve, veteran, recruit, and cadet, and for all branches of service. I pray you find encouragement in the scriptures. I chose each Bible verse to provide God's words for protection, power, and perseverance. Tightly grip onto each promise. Depend on them during times of need. Find hope. Remember His faithfulness. Carry this book with you everywhere and use it often.

Thank you for your honorable, dedicated, sacrificial service. Thank you for defending the freedoms we all enjoy today. And thank you to your families, who share in your sacrifice to our country.

God's blessings over you,

Nancy

FOR GOD DIDN'T GIVE US A
SPIRIT OF FEAR, BUT OF POWER,
LOVE, AND SELF-CONTROL.
2 TIMOTHY 1:7

2 Timothy 1:7 Spirit of Power, Love, Self-Control

2

NOT ONLY THIS, BUT WE ALSO
REJOICE IN OUR SUFFERINGS,
KNOWING THAT SUFFERING
PRODUCES PERSEVERANCE;
AND PERSEVERANCE, PROVEN
CHARACTER; AND PROVEN
CHARACTER, HOPE: AND HOPE
DOESN'T DISAPPOINT US, BECAUSE
GOD'S LOVE HAS BEEN POURED
INTO OUR HEARTS THROUGH THE
HOLY SPIRIT WHO WAS GIVEN
TO US.
Romans 5:3-5

Romans 5:3-5 Perseverance, Character, Hope

THEREFORE PUT ON THE WHOLE ARMOR
OF GOD, THAT YOU MAY BE ABLE TO
WITHSTAND IN THE EVIL DAY, AND HAVING
DONE ALL, TO STAND. STAND THEREFORE,
HAVING THE UTILITY BELT OF TRUTH
BUCKLED AROUND YOUR WAIST, AND
HAVING PUT ON THE BREASTPLATE OF
RIGHTEOUSNESS, AND HAVING FITTED YOUR
FEET WITH THE PREPARATION OF THE
GOOD NEWS OF PEACE, ABOVE ALL, TAKING
UP THE SHIELD OF FAITH, WITH WHICH YOU
WILL BE ABLE TO QUENCH ALL THE FIERY
DARTS OF THE EVIL ONE. AND TAKE THE
HELMET OF SALVATION, AND THE SWORD OF
THE SPIRIT, WHICH IS THE WORD OF GOD;
WITH ALL PRAYER AND REQUESTS, PRAYING
AT ALL TIMES IN THE SPIRIT.
Ephesians 6:14-18

Ephesians 6:14-18 Whole Armor of God

HONOR ALL MEN. LOVE THE BROTHERHOOD. FEAR GOD.

1 Peter 2:17

1 Peter 2:17 Honor Men, Love Brotherhood, Fear God

I HAVE TOLD YOU THESE THINGS, THAT IN ME YOU MAY HAVE PEACE. IN THE WORLD YOU HAVE TROUBLE; BUT CHEER UP! I HAVE OVERCOME THE WORLD.

John 16:33

John 16:33 I Have Overcome the World

BUT THANKS BE TO GOD,
WHO GIVES US THE VICTORY
THROUGH OUR LORD JESUS CHRIST.
THEREFORE, MY BELOVED
BROTHERS, BE STEADFAST,
IMMOVABLE, ALWAYS ABOUNDING
IN THE LORD'S WORK, BECAUSE
YOU KNOW THAT YOUR LABOR IS
NOT IN VAIN IN THE LORD.
1 Corinthians 15:57-58

1 Corinthians 15:57-58 Steadfast, Immovable, Abounding in Lord's Work

THIS HOPE WE HAVE AS AN ANCHOR OF THE SOUL, A HOPE BOTH SURE AND STEADFAST.
Hebrews 6:19

Hebrews 6:19 Anchor of the Soul

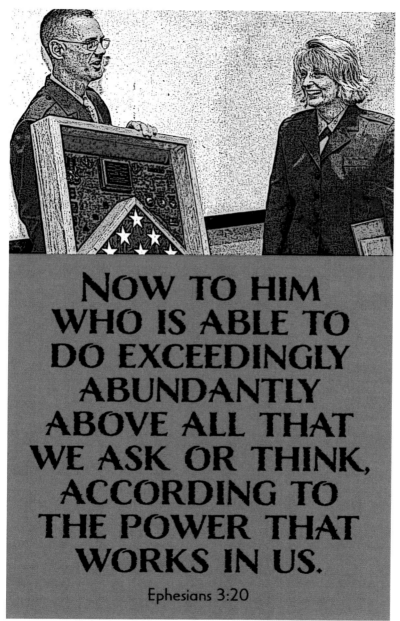

NOW TO HIM WHO IS ABLE TO DO EXCEEDINGLY ABUNDANTLY ABOVE ALL THAT WE ASK OR THINK, ACCORDING TO THE POWER THAT WORKS IN US.

Ephesians 3:20

Ephesians 3:20 Exceedingly Abundantly Above

AND WHATEVER YOU
DO, WORK HEARTILY,
AS FOR THE LORD,
AND NOT FOR MEN,
KNOWING THAT FROM
THE LORD YOU WILL
RECEIVE THE REWARD
OF THE INHERITANCE;
FOR YOU SERVE THE
LORD CHRIST.
Colossians 3:23-24

Colossians 3:23-24 Work Heartily as For the Lord

HAVEN'T I COMMANDED YOU? BE STRONG AND COURAGEOUS. DON'T BE AFRAID. DON'T BE DISMAYED, FOR THE LORD YOUR GOD IS WITH YOU WHEREVER YOU GO.

Joshua 1:9

Joshua 1:9 Be Strong and Courageous

GOD IS OUR REFUGE AND STRENGTH, A VERY PRESENT HELP IN TROUBLE.

Psalm 46:1

Psalm 46:1 Refuge, Strength, Help in Trouble

LET'S THEREFORE DRAW NEAR WITH BOLDNESS TO THE THRONE OF GRACE, THAT WE MAY RECEIVE MERCY AND MAY FIND GRACE FOR HELP IN TIME OF NEED.
Hebrews 4:16

Hebrews 4:16 Receive Mercy and Grace in Time of Need

2 Samuel 22:40 Armed Me with Strength

THE LORD WILL GUARD YOUR GOING AND COMING.
Psalm 121:8

Psalm 121:8 Lord Will Guard Going and Coming

THE LORD BLESS YOU, AND KEEP YOU.
THE LORD MAKE HIS FACE TO SHINE ON
YOU, AND BE GRACIOUS TO YOU. THE
LORD LIFT UP HIS FACE TOWARD YOU,
AND GIVE YOU PEACE.
Numbers 6:24-26

Numbers 6:24-26 The Lord Bless You

TRUST IN THE LORD WITH ALL YOUR HEART, AND DON'T LEAN ON YOUR OWN UNDERSTANDING. IN ALL YOUR WAYS ACKNOWLEDGE HIM, AND HE WILL MAKE YOUR PATHS STRAIGHT.

Proverbs 3:5-6

Proverbs 3:5-6 He Will Make Your Paths Straight

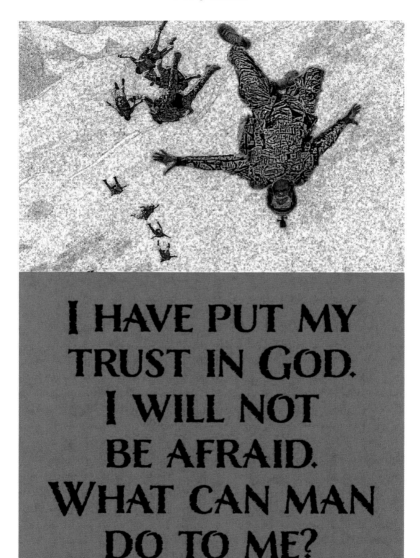

I HAVE PUT MY TRUST IN GOD. I WILL NOT BE AFRAID. WHAT CAN MAN DO TO ME?

Psalm 56:11

Psalm 56:11 What Can Man Do to Me?

Isaiah 6:8 Here I Am. Send Me

GOD IS WITHIN HER. SHE SHALL NOT BE MOVED. GOD WILL HELP HER AT DAWN.
Psalm 46:5

Psalm 46:5 She Shall Not Be Moved

BUT IF ANY OF YOU LACKS WISDOM,
LET HIM ASK OF GOD, WHO GIVES TO ALL
LIBERALLY AND WITHOUT REPROACH,
AND IT WILL BE GIVEN TO HIM.
James 1:5

James 1:5 Ask God for Wisdom

"FOR I KNOW THE THOUGHTS THAT I THINK TOWARD YOU," SAYS THE LORD, "THOUGHTS OF PEACE, AND NOT OF EVIL, TO GIVE YOU HOPE AND A FUTURE. YOU SHALL CALL ON ME, AND YOU SHALL GO AND PRAY TO ME, AND I WILL LISTEN TO YOU. YOU SHALL SEEK ME, AND FIND ME, WHEN YOU SEARCH FOR ME WITH ALL YOUR HEART."
Jeremiah 29:11-13

Jeremiah 29:11-13 For I Know

THE LORD IS MY SHEPHERD: I SHALL LACK NOTHING. HE MAKES ME LIE DOWN IN GREEN PASTURES. HE LEADS ME BESIDE STILL WATER. HE RESTORES MY SOUL. HE GUIDES ME IN THE PATHS OF RIGHTEOUSNESS FOR HIS NAME'S SAKE. EVEN THOUGH I WALK THROUGH THE VALLEY OF THE SHADOW OF DEATH, I WILL FEAR NO EVIL, FOR YOU ARE WITH ME. YOUR ROD AND YOUR STAFF, THEY COMFORT ME. YOU PREPARE A TABLE BEFORE ME IN THE PRESENCE OF MY ENEMIES. YOU ANOINT MY HEAD WITH OIL. MY CUP RUNS OVER. SURELY GOODNESS AND LOVING KINDNESS SHALL FOLLOW ME ALL THE DAYS OF MY LIFE, AND I WILL DWELL IN THE LORD'S HOUSE FOREVER.
Psalm 23:1-10

Psalm 23:1-10 The Lord is My Shepherd

1 John 4:4 Greater Is He Who Is in You

NOW MAY THE GOD OF HOPE FILL YOU
WITH ALL JOY AND PEACE IN BELIEVING,
THAT YOU MAY ABOUND IN HOPE,
IN THE POWER OF THE HOLY SPIRIT.
Romans 15:13

Romans 15:13 Joy, Peace, Hope, Power of Holy Spirit

THIS I RECALL TO MY MIND;
THEREFORE I HAVE HOPE. IT IS
BECAUSE OF THE LORD'S LOVING
KINDNESSES THAT WE ARE NOT
CONSUMED, BECAUSE HIS
COMPASSION DOESN'T FAIL. THEY
ARE NEW EVERY MORNING.
GREAT IS YOUR FAITHFULNESS.
"THE LORD IS MY PORTION," SAYS
MY SOUL. "THEREFORE I WILL
HOPE IN HIM."
Lamentations 3:21-25

Lamentations 3:21-25 Great Is Your Faithfulness

BUT THE FRUIT OF THE SPIRIT IS LOVE, JOY, PEACE, PATIENCE, KINDNESS, GOODNESS, FAITH, GENTLENESS, AND SELF-CONTROL. AGAINST SUCH THINGS THERE IS NO LAW.

Galatians 5:22-23

Galatians 5:22-23 Fruit of the Spirit

DON'T BE AFRAID, FOR I HAVE
REDEEMED YOU. I HAVE CALLED
YOU BY YOUR NAME. YOU ARE
MINE. WHEN YOU PASS THROUGH
THE WATER, I WILL BE WITH YOU,
AND THROUGH THE RIVERS, THEY
WILL NOT OVERFLOW YOU. WHEN
YOU WALK THROUGH THE FIRE,
YOU WILL NOT BE BURNED, AND
FLAME WILL NOT SCORCH YOU.
Isaiah 43:1-2

Isaiah 43:1-2 When You Pass Through Water, I Will Be with You

WATCH! STAND FIRM IN THE FAITH! BE COURAGEOUS! BE STRONG!
1 Corinthians 16:13

1 Corinthians 16:13 Stand Firm in the Faith!

BUT GLORY, HONOR, AND PEACE GO TO EVERY MAN WHO DOES GOOD.

Romans 2:10

Romans 2:10 Glory, Honor, Peace

WE KNOW THAT ALL THINGS WORK TOGETHER
FOR GOOD FOR THOSE WHO LOVE GOD,
FOR THOSE WHO ARE CALLED ACCORDING TO
HIS PURPOSE. FOR WHOM HE FOREKNEW, HE
ALSO PREDESTINED TO BE CONFORMED TO THE
IMAGE OF HIS SON, THAT HE MIGHT BE THE
FIRSTBORN AMONG MANY BROTHERS. WHOM
HE PREDESTINED, THOSE HE ALSO CALLED.
WHOM HE CALLED, THOSE HE ALSO JUSTIFIED.
WHOM HE JUSTIFIED, THOSE HE ALSO GLORIFIED.
WHAT THEN SHALL WE SAY ABOUT THESE
IF GOD IS FOR US, WHO CAN BE AGAINST US?
Romans 8:28-31

Romans 8:28-31 If God is For Us, Who Can Be Against?

WHO SHALL SEPARATE US FROM THE
LOVE OF CHRIST? COULD OPPRESSION,
OR ANGUISH, OR PERSECUTION, OR
FAMINE, OR NAKEDNESS, OR PERIL, OR
SWORD? NO, IN ALL THESE THINGS,
WE ARE MORE THAN CONQUERORS
THROUGH HIM WHO LOVED US. FOR I AM
PERSUADED THAT NEITHER DEATH, NOR
LIFE, NOR ANGELS, NOR PRINCIPALITIES,
NOR THINGS PRESENT, NOR THINGS TO
COME, NOR POWERS, NOR HEIGHT, NOR
DEPTH, NOR ANY OTHER CREATED THING
WILL BE ABLE TO SEPARATE US FROM
GOD'S LOVE WHICH IS IN
CHRIST JESUS OUR LORD.
Romans 8:35, 37-39

Romans 8:35, 37-39 Who Shall Separate Us from Christ?

TWO ARE BETTER THAN ONE,
BECAUSE THEY HAVE A GOOD
REWARD FOR THEIR LABOR. FOR
IF THEY FALL, THE ONE WILL LIFT
UP HIS FELLOW; IF A MAN
PREVAILS AGAINST ONE WHO IS
ALONE, TWO SHALL WITHSTAND
HIM; AND A THREEFOLD CORD IS
NOT QUICKLY BROKEN.

Ecclesiastes 4:9-10, 12

Ecclesiastes 4:9-10, 12 Threefold Cord Not Quickly Broken

SOME TRUST IN CHARIOTS, AND SOME IN HORSES, BUT WE TRUST IN THE NAME OF THE LORD OUR GOD. THEY ARE BOWED DOWN AND FALLEN, BUT WE RISE UP, AND STAND UPRIGHT.

Psalm 20:7-8

Psalm 20:7-8 Rise Up, Stand Upright

FOR BODILY EXERCISE HAS SOME VALUE, BUT GODLINESS HAS VALUE IN ALL THINGS, HAVING THE PROMISE OF THE LIFE WHICH IS NOW, AND OF THAT WHICH IS TO COME.

1 Timothy 4:8

1 Timothy 4:8 Bodily Exercise

HE WHO FOLLOWS AFTER RIGHTEOUSNESS AND KINDNESS FINDS LIFE, RIGHEOUSNESS, AND HONOR.
Proverbs 21:21

Proverbs 21:21 Life, Righteousness, Honor

You will keep whoever's mind is steadfast in perfect peace, because he trusts in you. Trust in the Lord forever; for in the Lord, the Lord, is an everlasting Rock. Now may the Lord of peace himself give you peace at all times in all ways. The Lord be with you all.

Isaiah 26:3-4

Isaiah 26:3-4 Mind in Perfect Peace

WE ARE PRESSED ON
EVERY SIDE, YET NOT
CRUSHED; PERPLEXED,
YET NOT TO DESPAIR;
PURSUED, YET NOT
FORSAKEN; STRUCK
DOWN, YET NOT
DESTROYED.
2 Corinthians 4:8-9

2 Corinthians 4:8-9 Pressed, Not Crushed

LORD, GOD OF ARMIES, WHO IS A MIGHTY ONE, LIKE YOU? YOU RULE THE PRIDE OF THE SEA. WHEN ITS WAVES RISE UP, YOU CALM THEM.
Psalm 89:8-9

Psalm 89:8-9 Calm the Waves

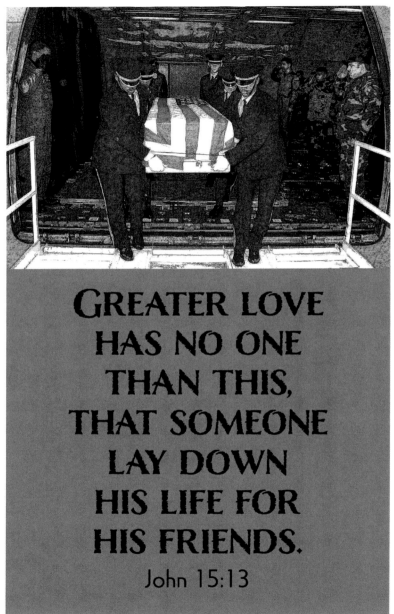

GREATER LOVE HAS NO ONE THAN THIS, THAT SOMEONE LAY DOWN HIS LIFE FOR HIS FRIENDS.
John 15:13

John 15:13 Lay Down Life for Friends

BE STILL, AND KNOW THAT I AM GOD.
I WILL BE EXALTED AMONG THE NATIONS.
I WILL BE EXALTED IN THE EARTH.
Psalm 46:10

Psalm 46:10 Be Still and Know that I Am God

IN THE MULTITUDE
OF MY THOUGHTS
WITHIN ME, YOUR
COMFORTS DELIGHT
MY SOUL.
Psalm 94:19

Psalm 94:19 In the Multitude of My Thoughts

BY AWESOME DEEDS OF
RIGHTEOUSNESS, YOU ANSWER US,
GOD OF OUR SALVATION.
YOU WHO ARE THE HOPE OF ALL THE
ENDS OF THE EARTH, OF THOSE WHO
ARE FAR AWAY ON THE SEA.
BY YOUR POWER, YOU FORM THE
MOUNTAINS, HAVING ARMED
YOURSELF WITH STRENGTH. YOU STILL
THE ROARING OF THE SEAS, THE
ROARING OF THEIR WAVES, AND THE
TURMOIL OF THE NATIONS.

Psalm 65:5-7

Psalm 65:5-7 Those Who Are Far Away on the Sea

HE GIVES POWER TO THE WEAK. HE INCREASES THE STRENGTH OF HIM WHO HAS NO MIGHT. EVEN THE YOUTHS FAINT AND GET WEARY, AND THE YOUNG MEN UTTERLY FALL; THE LORD WILL RENEW THEIR STRENGTH. THEY WILL MOUNT UP WITH WINGS LIKE EAGLES. THEY WILL RUN, AND NOT BE WEARY. THEY WILL WALK, AND NOT FAINT.

Isaiah 40:29-31

Isaiah 40:29-31 Mount Up with Wings Like Eagles

AND GOD IS ABLE TO
MAKE ALL GRACE
ABOUND TO YOU, THAT
YOU, ALWAYS HAVING
ALL SUFFICIENCY IN
EVERYTHING, MAY
ABOUND TO EVERY
GOOD WORK.
2 Corinthians 9:8

2 Corinthians 9:8 Abound to Every Good Work

FOR WHO IS GOD, EXCEPT THE LORD?
WHO IS A ROCK, BESIDES OUR GOD,
THE GOD WHO ARMS ME WITH STRENGTH,
AND MAKES MY WAY PERFECT?
HE MAKES MY FEET LIKE DEER'S FEET,
AND SETS ME ON MY HIGH PLACES.
HE TEACHES MY HANDS TO WAR,
SO THAT MY ARMS BEND A BOW OF BRONZE.
YOU HAVE ALSO GIVEN ME THE SHIELD
OF YOUR SALVATION. YOU HAVE ALSO
GIVEN ME THE SHIELD OF YOUR SALVATION.
YOUR RIGHT HAND SUSTAINS ME.
YOUR GENTLENESS HAS MADE ME GREAT.
YOU HAVE ENLARGED MY STEPS UNDER ME.

Psalm 18:31-36

Psalm 18:31-36 He Teaches My Hands to War

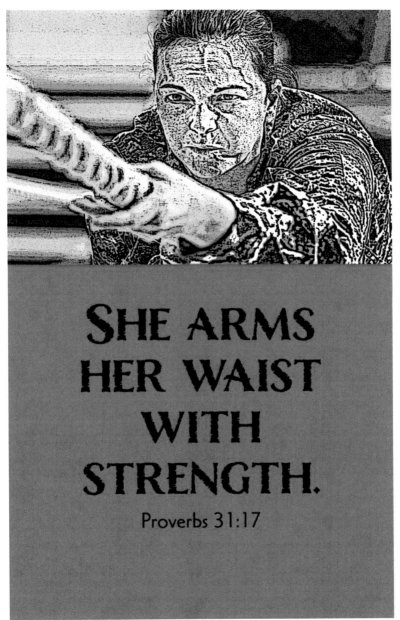

SHE ARMS HER WAIST WITH STRENGTH.

Proverbs 31:17

Proverbs 31:17 She Arms Her Waist with Strength

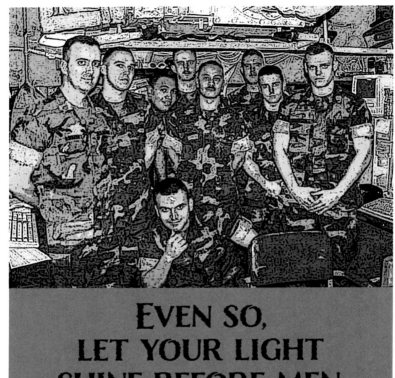

EVEN SO, LET YOUR LIGHT SHINE BEFORE MEN, THAT THEY MAY SEE YOUR GOOD WORKS AND GLORIFY YOUR FATHER WHO IS IN HEAVEN.
Matthew 5:16

Matthew 5:16 Light Shine Before Men

BEING CONFIDENT OF THIS VERY THING, THAT HE WHO BEGAN A GOOD WORK IN YOU WILL COMPLETE IT UNTIL THE DAY OF JESUS CHRIST.

Philippians 1:6

Philippians 1:6 He Who Began a Good Work in You

THE LORD SAYS TO YOU, "DON'T BE AFRAID, AND DON'T BE DISMAYED BECAUSE OF THIS GREAT MULTITUDE; FOR THE BATTLE IS NOT YOURS, BUT GOD'S."

2 Chronicles 20:15

2 Chronicles 20:15 Battle is Not Yours, But God's

GLORY TO GOD IN THE HIGHEST, ON EARTH PEACE, GOOD WILL TOWARD MEN.

Luke 2:14

Luke 2:14 Peace on Earth, Good Will Toward Men

FOR EVERYTHING THERE IS A SEASON, A TIME FOR EVERY PURPOSE UNDER HEAVEN: A TIME TO BE BORN, AND A TIME TO DIE; A TIME TO PLANT, AND A TIME TO PLUCK UP THAT WHICH IS PLANTED; A TIME TO KILL, A TIME TO HEAL; A TIME TO BREAK DOWN, AND A TIME TO BUILD UP; A TIME TO WEEP, AND A TIME TO LAUGH; A TIME TO MOURN, AND A TIME TO DANCE; A TIME TO CAST AWAY STONES, AND A TIME TO GATHER STONES TOGETER; A TIME TO EMBRACE, AND A TIME TO REFRAIN FROM EMBRACING; A TIME TO SEEK, AND A TIME TO LOSE; A TIME TO KEEP, AND A TIME TO CAST AWAY; A TIME TO TEAR, AND A TIME TO SEW; A TIME TO KEEP SILENCE, AND A TIME TO SPEAK; A TIME TO LOVE, AND A TIME TO HATE; A TIME FOR WAR, AND A TIME FOR PEACE.
Ecclesiastes 3:1-8

Ecclesiastes 3:1-8 For Everything There is A Season

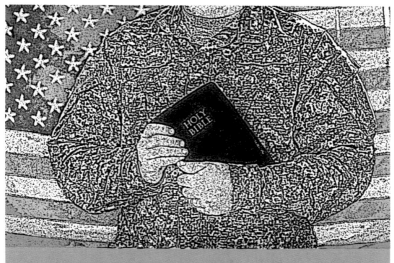

DON'T YOU BE AFRAID, FOR I AM WITH YOU. DON'T BE DISMAYED, FOR I AM YOUR GOD. I WILL STRENGTHEN YOU. YES, I WILL HELP YOU. YES, I WILL UPHOLD YOU WITH THE RIGHT HAND OF MY RIGHTEOUSNESS.
Isaiah 41:10

Isaiah 41:10 I Will Strengthen You

THE LORD WILL FIGHT FOR YOU, AND YOU SHALL BE STILL.

Exodus 14:14

Exodus 14:14 Lord Will Fight for You

Psalm 119:114 Hiding Place and Shield

"NO WEAPON THAT IS FORMED AGAINST YOU WILL PREVAIL; AND YOU WILL CONDEMN EVERY TONGUE THAT RISES AGAINST YOU IN JUDGMENT. THIS IS THE HERITAGE OF THE LORD'S SERVANTS, AND THEIR RIGHTEOUSNESS IS OF ME," SAYS THE LORD.

Isaiah 54:17

Isaiah 54:17 No Weapon Formed Against You Will Prevail

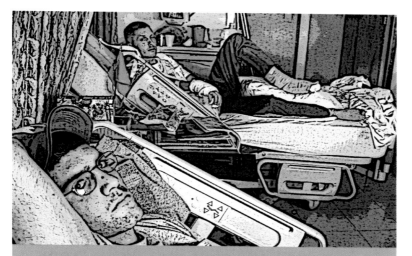

"COME TO ME, ALL YOU WHO
LABOR AND ARE HEAVILY
BURDENED, AND I WILL GIVE
YOU REST. TAKE MY YOKE
UPON YOU AND LEARN FROM
ME, FOR I AM GENTLE AND
HUMBLE IN HEART; AND YOU
WILL FIND REST FOR YOUR
SOULS. FOR MY YOKE IS EASY,
AND MY BURDEN IS LIGHT."
Matthew 11:28-30

Matthew 11:28-30 My Yoke Is Easy, My Burden Is Light

NOT THAT I SPEAK BECAUSE OF
LACK, FOR I HAVE LEARNED IN
WHATEVER STATE I AM, TO BE
CONTENT IN IT. I KNOW HOW TO
BE HUMBLED, AND I ALSO KNOW
HOW TO ABOUND. IN EVERYTHING
AND IN ALL THINGS I HAVE
LEARNED THE SECRET BOTH TO BE
FILLED AND TO BE HUNGRY, BOTH
TO ABOUND AND TO BE IN NEED.
I CAN DO ALL THINGS THROUGH
CHRIST, WHO STRENGTHENS ME.

Philippians 4:11-13

Philippians 4:11-13 I Can Do All Things Through Christ

I HAVE FOUGHT THE GOOD FIGHT. I HAVE FINISHED THE COURSE. I HAVE KEPT THE FAITH.

2 Timothy 4:7

2 Timothy 4:7 Fought the Good Fight

IN LOVE OF THE BROTHERS
BE TENDERLY AFFECTIONATE
TO ONE ANOTHER; IN HONOR
PREFERRING ONE ANOTHER;
NOT LAGGING IN DILIGENCE;
FERVENT IN SPIRIT; SERVING
THE LORD; REJOICING IN HOPE;
ENDURING IN TROUBLES;
CONTINUING STEADFASTLY
IN PRAYER.
Romans 12:10-12

Romans 12:10-12 In Honor Preferring One Another

A MAN OF MANY COMPANIONS MAY BE RUINED, BUT THERE IS A FRIEND WHO STICKS CLOSER THAN A BROTHER.

Proverbs 18:24

Proverbs 18:24 Friend Sticks Closer Than Brother

Ephesians 2:10 Created in Christ Jesus for Good Works

THEREFORE I URGE YOU, BROTHERS,
BY THE MERCIES OF GOD, TO PRESENT
YOUR BODIES A LIVING SACRIFICE, HOLY,
ACCEPTABLE TO GOD, WHICH IS YOUR
SPIRITUAL SERVICE. DON'T BE
CONFORMED TO THIS WORLD, BUT BE
TRANSFORMED BY THE RENEWING OF
YOUR MIND, SO THAT YOU MAY PROVE
WHAT IS THE GOOD, WELL-PLEASING,
AND PERFECT WILL OF GOD.
Romans 12:1-2

Romans 12:1-2 Renewing of Your Mind

BUT HE WAS
PIERCED FOR OUR
TRANSGRESSIONS.
HE WAS CRUSHED
FOR OUR INIQUITIES.
THE PUNISHMENT
THAT BROUGHT OUR
PEACE WAS ON HIM;
AND BY HIS WOUNDS
WE ARE HEALED.
Isaiah 53:5

Isaiah 53:5 By His Wounds We Are Healed

HEAR MY CRY, GOD.
LISTEN TO MY PRAYER.
FROM THE END OF THE EARTH,
I WILL CALL TO YOU WHEN
MY HEART IS OVERWHELMED.
LEAD ME TO THE ROCK THAT IS
HIGHER THAN I. FOR YOU
HAVE BEEN A REFUGE FOR ME,
A STRONG TOWER FROM THE ENEMY.
I WILL DWELL IN YOUR TENT FOREVER.
I WILL TAKE REFUGE IN THE
SHELTER OF YOUR WINGS.

Psalm 61:1-4

Psalm 61:1-4 Strong Tower from the Enemy

65

I WILL IN NO WAY LEAVE YOU, NEITHER WILL I IN ANY WAY FORSAKE YOU.

Hebrews 13:5

Hebrews 13:5 I Will in No Way Leave You

THE LORD GOD'S SPIRIT IS ON ME, BECAUSE THE LORD
HAS ANOINTED ME TO PREACH GOOD NEWS TO THE
HUMBLE. HE HAS SENT ME TO BIND UP THE BROKEN
HEARTED, TO PROCLAIM LIBERTY TO THE CAPTIVES AND
RELEASE TO THOSE WHO ARE BOUND, TO PROCLAIM THE
YEAR OF THE LORD'S FAVOR AND THE DAY OF VENGEANCE
OF OUR GOD, TO COMFORT ALL WHO MOURN, TO PROVIDE
FOR THOSE WHO MOURN IN ZION, TO GIVE TO THEM A
GARLAND FOR ASHES, THE OIL OF JOY FOR MOURNING, THE
GARMENT OF PRAISE FOR THE SPIRIT OF HEAVINESS, THAT
THEY MAY BE CALLED TREES OF RIGHTEOUSNESS, THE
PLANTING OF THE LORD, THAT HE MAY BE GLORIFIED.
Isaiah 61:1-3

Isaiah 61:1-3 Oil of Joy for Mourning

I EXHORT THEREFORE, FIRST OF ALL, THAT
PETITIONS, PRAYERS, INTERCESSIONS,
AND GIVINGS OF THANKS BE MADE FOR ALL
MEN: FOR KINGS AND ALL WHO ARE IN HIGH
PLACES, THAT WE MAY LEAD A TRANQUIL
AND QUIET LIFE IN ALL GODLINESS AND
REVERENCE.
1 Timothy 2:1-2

1 Timothy 2:1-2 That We May Lead a Tranquil and Quiet Life

REJOICE IN THE LORD ALWAYS! AGAIN I WILL SAY,
"REJOICE!" LET YOUR GENTLENESS BE KNOWN TO ALL
MEN. THE LORD IS AT HAND. IN NOTHING BE ANXIOUS,
BUT IN EVERYTHING, BY PRAYER AND PETITION WITH
THANKSGIVING, LET YOUR REQUESTS BE MADE
KNOWN TO GOD. AND THE PEACE OF GOD, WHICH
SURPASSES ALL UNDERSTANDING, WILL GUARD YOUR
HEARTS AND YOUR THOUGHTS IN CHRIST JESUS.
FINALLY, BROTHERS, WHATEVER THINGS ARE TRUE,
WHATEVER THINGS ARE HONORABLE, WHATEVER
THINGS ARE JUST, WHATEVER THINGS ARE PURE,
WHATEVER THINGS ARE LOVELY, WHATEVER THINGS
ARE OF GOOD REPORT: IF THERE IS ANY VIRTUE AND
IF THERE IS ANY PRAISE, THINK ABOUT THESE THINGS.
Philippians 4:4-8

Philippians 4:4-8 Peace of God Which Surpasses Understanding

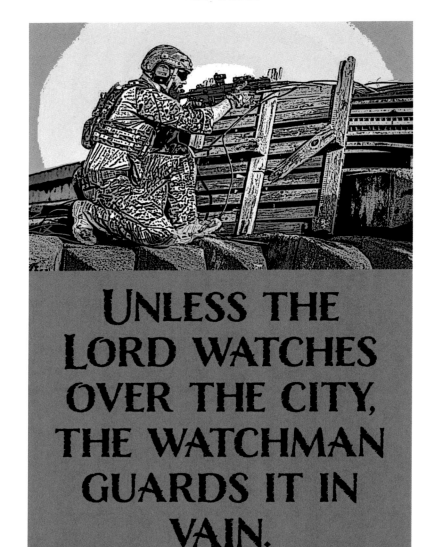

Psalm 127:1 Unless the Lord Watches Over City

IN PEACE I WILL BOTH LAY MYSELF DOWN AND SLEEP, FOR YOU, LORD ALONE, MAKE ME LIVE IN SAFETY.
Psalm 4:8

Psalm 4:8 In Peace I Lay Down and Sleep

Psalm 35:1 Contend with Those Who Contend with Me

NOW THE LORD IS THE SPIRIT, AND WHERE THE SPIRIT OF THE LORD IS, THERE IS FREEDOM.

2 Corinthians 3:17

2 Corinthians 3:17 Where Spirit of the Lord Is, There is Freedom

LET EVERY SOUL BE IN SUBJECTION TO
THE HIGHER AUTHORITIES, FOR THERE IS
NO AUTHORITY EXCEPT FROM GOD,
AND THOSE WHO EXIST ARE ORDAINED
BY GOD.

FOR RULERS ARE NOT A TERROR TO THE
GOOD WORK, DO THAT WHICH IS GOOD,
AND YOU WILL HAVE PRAISE FROM THE
AUTHORITY, FOR HE IS A SERVANT OF
GOD TO YOU FOR GOOD.

Romans 13:1, 3-4

Romans 13:1, 3-4 Subjection to Higher Authority

HE WHO RESPECTS A COMMAND WILL BE REWARDED.

Proverbs 13:13

Proverbs 13:13 He Who Respects a Command

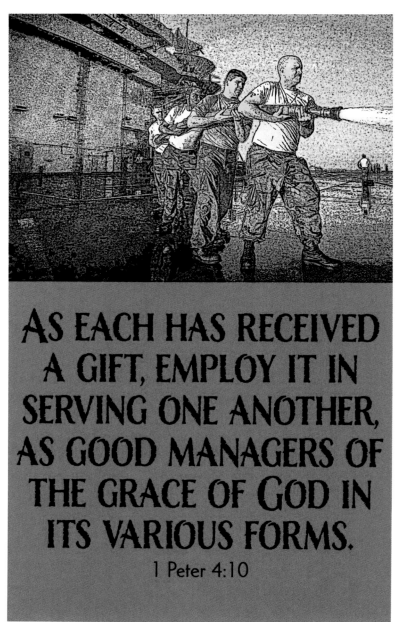

AS EACH HAS RECEIVED
A GIFT, EMPLOY IT IN
SERVING ONE ANOTHER,
AS GOOD MANAGERS OF
THE GRACE OF GOD IN
ITS VARIOUS FORMS.
1 Peter 4:10

1 Peter 4:10 Serving One Another

Psalm 68:19 Lord Daily Bears Our Burdens

ABOUT THE AUTHOR

Nancy DeJesus lives in Virginia with her husband. They have seven children and two grandchildren. She has a B.S. in Art Education from the Pennsylvania State University. She taught art in the public schools and is a Visual Art Subject Matter Specialist for a homeschool company. She is devoted to her local church.

Nancy is a small business owner. She sells her books and photographs on www.NancyDeJesusPhotography.com.

ACKNOWLEDGEMENTS

Thank you to Mannie D., Felipe B., Angel R., Alba R., Hilda T., Andres T., Norma F-T., Carlos P., Liberty R., Danny R., Frankie R., Jimmy R., Bryant D., Bret H., David B., Jeremy G., Scott P., Doreen B., Bobby H., Rob C., Abby C., Bethany C., John A., and everyone who serves or has served in the military. Thank you to Mannie for being a wonderfully supportive husband and to my family for understanding the calling and passion God placed on my heart to use my photography and writing to help others.

OTHER TITLES BY THE AUTHOR

Heart to Heart · Scripture and Prayer Journals
Volume 1: Heart and Mind Transformations
Volume 2: Trials and Suffering
Volume 3: Relationships ~ Love God, Love People
Volume 4: Fruit of the Spirit

Memoirs of the Funniest Little Man of God
Volume 1: Macario 2 to 4 Years Old
Volume 2: Macario 5 to 6 Years Old

Speak Life into Your Life by Declaring God's Promises
Speak Life into Your Life by Declaring God's Promises
For Teens ~ Speak Life into Your Life by Declaring God's Promises
For Men ~ Speak Life into Your Life by Declaring God's Promises

Scripture with Pictures
Volume 1: Old Testament Verses on Images of God's Creation
Volume 2: New Testament Verses on Images of God's Creation

.

Made in the USA
Middletown, DE
05 July 2021

43616030R00049